too-loose the
chocolate moose
30th Anniversary Edition
by *Stewart Moskowitz*

Published by Stewart Moskowitz Media
First edition for print, ISBN: 978-0985146719
Original edition published in 1982 by Simon & Schuster, New York

Once upon a time, far off in the Canadian woods, there lived a Momma and Poppa Moose whose favorite food in all the world was chocolate.

They ate nothing but chocolate, chocolate, and more chocolate!

Well, one day Momma and Poppa Moose had a baby moose who they called Too-loose. But this was no ordinary, everyday baby moose. This was a...

...CHOCOLATE MOOSE! Yes, Too-loose, the Chocolate Moose. That's right: the baby moose was made of chocolate. From the tips of his hooves to the ends of his antlers, he was solid chocolate.

Now, you might say "Wow!" or even "Yum Yum". But not so for Too-loose the Chocolate Moose. Life is not easy when you are made of chocolate.

He tried to play hide-n-seek.
But all the other mooses had only to follow the
trail of chocolate to find Too-loose.

He tried to play baseball with the other mooses,
but he got the ball all sticky.

He couldn't play leapfrog because he was
just too slippery.

So Too-loose led a singularly solitary life. Most days, he just sat by the stream and dreamed about what he would do with himself.

He couldn't be a symphony conductor.
Every time he'd wave the baton,
he'd splatter chocolate on the violins.

He couldn't be an astronaut.
He'd slide right out of the spaceship!

He couldn't work in the steel mills.
He'd melt into syrup in all of that heat.
Poor Too-loose! He was afraid he wasn't
good for anything.

And so, feeling down and out,
he went for a walk in the woods thinking,
"What can I be?"
He was so lost in his sad thoughts
that he didn't watch where he was going
and sure enough...

...he slipped right in his own chocolate...

...and somersaulted right through Auntie Moose's open kitchen window onto her table.

"Look what you've done!" cried Auntie Moose.
"You have ruined my pudding! What am I to do?"

"Don't worry,
Auntie. I'll make up a new
batch for you right away!"
said Too-loose.
So he started mixing
ingredients (naturally dripping
gobs and gobs of chocolate
right into the batter) and lo
and behold...
he was soon
finished with
a bowl of...
stuff!

Auntie Moose was the first to taste it.
She said: "Wow! Yum yum!
You ought to become a dessert maker!"

"That's it!" said Too-loose. "I'll become a dessert maker!"
And he did. Now Too-loose is famous the world over for
his stuff, which he named after himself: Chocolate Moose,
of course!